Murder Gone Viral

Stephen Simpson

First published in eBook as Viral on 8 December 2012

ISBN 9798574962442
Printed, bound, and distributed by Amazon KDP

Language: British English

Cover created with Canva.com

Independently published by Fiction for the Soul.

This edition is also available in eBook and audio book.

www.stephensimpsonbooks.com

What readers are saying

- "Great read from a great author."
- "This author knows just how to pull the reader in."
- "The author takes you on a journey and as the reader you never want it to end!"

Stephen Simpson writes horror fiction with **gasp!** endings.

Stories from Fiction for the Soul

Horror by Stephen Simpson

- Chain Letter
- Murder Gone Viral
- The Invisible Girl in Room Thirteen
- What My Soul Does When I Am Asleep
- Zombie Girl series
  - UnDead Girl

Urban Fantasy by Rosaline Saul

- Blood Moon
- My Life Hereafter
- ForNever series
  - Timeless
  - A Shade of Witch
- The OtherWorld

Sweet Romance by Lynette Ferreira

- Pocketful of Hope
- The Great Divide
- The Shape of My Soul

- Samantha & The Empath
- Paper Hearts
- The Reaper
- Recycled Souls series
  - My Recycled Soul
  - When Destiny Collides
- Counting Stars series
  - Forever Young

Short Stories

- Would you Remember ME
- All Over Again
- Only in My Memories
- New Dawn
- In the End

Flash Fiction by Elizabeth van Heerden

- The Dark, Dark House
- Fifteen Seconds Ago
- My Child, My Life
- My Entry into the Abyss
- The Beginning of a Life Misunderstood
- The Tokolosh
- GASP!
- Remember When
- Never Forgotten

Murder Gone Viral

Stephen Simpson

ONE

"I want to be the next internet sensation."

Bored with Facebook and Twitter, envious of YouTube videos getting in excess of eight million views, Richard pushes his palms against the edge of his desk and shoves himself away from his desktop. The wheels under his chair swivel the chair backwards until it hooks onto the bedside rug behind him. Despondently he wonders when it will be his turn. He is tired of waiting for his fifteen seconds of fame.

He spins around in the chair and looks across his Ivy League college dorm room at Gareth sitting up on his bed, his back against the wall behind him and his earphones

plugged into his ears.

Richard leans across the empty space between him and the desk and grabs hold of his substantial and chunky chemistry book. Holding the book in the air above his head, Richard hurls it at Gareth.

The book hits Gareth against the head and falls onto his lap, knocking the mug of coffee in his hand across the bed.

Gareth pulls the earphones from his ears and Richard hears the heavy metal from across the room. Agitated Gareth jumps up from the bed. "What the hell, Richard. What is your problem?" He exclaims in rage.

Richard grins. "I said, I want to be the next internet sensation."

"And why is that my problem? Look at the mess you made!" Gareth pulls his T-shirt over his head and starts to dab at the coffee puddles on his duvet.

Jokingly Richard explains, "You are the computer geek and together we can make it happen."

Irritated Gareth scoffs, "Why don't you go out and sit on the side-walk and wait for someone to get knocked over by a car or a bus and then upload that?"

"No. It must be memorable. I want to be remembered forever as the most infamous internet sensation ever in the history of the internet."

Gareth glances across his shoulder at Richard and he says tentatively, "I have been thinking about this one thing, but you will have to give up everything else and nobody can ever know it is you."

Richard sighs exasperated. "What would the use be of that?"

"You will know unless you need the acknowledgement from people, and you cannot just bask in your own glory."

Richard swivels the chair away from Gareth and looks at his computer screen. He opens his page and sneers when he sees the meagre twenty-five views on his page. It is for a video of Gareth sleeping, and him smearing shaving cream on his face and then tickling his nose. A juvenile, childish prank and it did not get the desired results he was hoping it would get. He sighs long and deeply. "I seriously want to be the next sensation. I want to upload a video that will go viral, and I will do anything to get it." He hesitates and glances across his shoulder at Gareth. "I will even sell my soul to the devil."

"If I tell you of my idea, you will have to sell your soul to the devil. This idea of mine is not for sissies."

Interested Richard turns back to Gareth. "So, are you going to tell me, or what?"

Gareth sits down on the edge of his bed and he leans his muscular forearms on his thighs. His expensive watch catches a glint from the overhead light. His hair is longish and light blond, brushed back casually from his forehead. He is dressed shabbily, but every piece of clothing on his body has a designer brand name.

He looks across the room at Richard pensively, measuring the distance between them and wondering if Richard will have the guts to go all the way with this unique idea. Although he is sure they could make millions of dollars with this idea, it would be too difficult to get their hands on the money. The path the money would have to follow to eventually get to them would be easily traceable, but if they only went for the hits and instant internet fame, it would be more difficult for the police to get a trace on them, especially if he buys and invests in the latest technologies to block his IP address and have the signal jumping around erratically. It was initially his

intention to do this all by himself, to be the one who becomes notorious. The one who fools the police for six days, before he disappears into oblivion, and then one day, sixty years from now, when he is too old to care whether he goes to jail or not, he will confess and become legendary overnight. He would be more well-known than the worst serial killer ever.

Richard interrupts his thoughts, “Are you going to tell me?”

Gareth smiles slowly. “You know all the reality shows there are on TV now? For singing, dancing, kissing, damn-well everything?”

“Yeah. Who doesn’t?”

“So, imagine if we got six kids. Let’s say, a high school football star, a homecoming queen, a scout, a junior baseball kid, a geek and an ordinary Joe, the options are endless. We follow and videotape them, but we have to get enough coverage to make a compelling thirty-second video.”

Richard says mockingly, “This sounds stupid. Do you honestly think we would become a global internet hit with such a lame idea?”

The look in Gareth's eyes turns sinister as he continues, "We abduct each kid and we keep them locked up for the six days, and each day the viewers of the online video must choose their favourite who will advance to the next day. The kids with the most votes will get another chance."

Richard frowns briefly and looks across the room at Gareth a little more interested.

"After we upload the video onto a fake, untraceable account that I will set up, we post the question: Which of these would you want to see tomorrow?" Gareth's voice becomes dramatic, like that of a reality show host. "Which one of these six kids do you think should live to see another day? Remember to cast your vote, because the one with the most votes will stay another day. So, be sure to vote for your favourite. If you do not vote, they will be out of the competition, all their dreams snuffed out like the flame of a candle."

Richard laughs, delighted. "We can make money from this."

Gareth looks at Richard derisively. "No. The police will be able to trace the money and will find you… us more

easily then. The money goes through your bank account eventually, dummy."

Nodding his head in understanding, Richards starts to smile. "What do you want me to do?"

"Are you sure you want to do this? Once we put this into motion there is no turning back."

"Hell yeah!" Richard cries out. "Of course, I want to do this. I cannot wait to sit here and see the view numbers on the computer screen roll over into the billions."

Gareth smiles cruelly. "And I can guarantee you the numbers will reach far into the billions. We will be the internet buzz for six glorious days."

Doubtfully Richard asks, "We aren't actually going to kill any of them, are we?"

"Now why would people bother to watch the second day's video if we do not show them the proof that one of them are dead? We will videotape and upload the losing kid's last screams."

Richard says perceptively, "That is why nobody can know it is us."

"So, let's make a list of all the things we need to do."

Gareth pulls a chair closer to Richard's desk and then

with their heads bend over the A4 sheet of paper, torn from a notebook, Gareth scribbles in his slanted handwriting the to-do list.

"Firstly, what type of contestants will we have?"

Richard rests his head onto his palm and taps with his index finger against his temple. "For the sympathy vote, we should have a girl of about seven to eight years of age."

Gareth writes it down onto the piece of paper. "To make our list ethnically correct, we should have a black kid as well."

Richard nods his head in agreement, and Gareth writes it down onto the list.

"I liked your earlier idea of the high school homecoming queen."

Gareth smiles as he adds it to the list. Under that he scribbles another contestant idea.

Richards smirks. "Almost forgot all about the all-important jock, the high school football hero." He laughs suddenly. "To make the list properly correct, we will have to have a disabled contestant."

"Brilliant, Richard. I never even considered that one. Then, for the contestant against all the odds, the ugliest

kid we can find."

Richard laughs heartily. "I am loving this idea." Abruptly he remembers, "Where are we going to keep them?"

"My dad has a hunting lodge an hour from here. This weekend we should go there and fix up the basement. It is quiet out there and there is not a living soul nearby for miles and miles."

Richard sighs exaggerated, a small smile playing on his lips. "Is this going to involve manual labour?"

"I will go to the hardware store and buy drywall, chains and anything else we could possibly need."

"Why drywall?"

"We want to lock them up separately. You do not want them to gang up against us. If they manage to escape and run to the police, you can kiss your chemical engineering degree goodbye."

"So, when do we start?"

"I will have to get some new gadgets and a new computer. Also, I will have to get some anti-tracking set-up. That will take me at least a week and with exams coming up it is going to be a tight schedule."

Enviously Richard sulks, “Your dad won’t get suspicious with you spending so much money?”

Gareth laughs derisively. “He is out of the country and when has he ever cared?” Gareth gets up from the chair and drags it behind him back to his side of the room. He pushes the chair under his desk and then he turns back to Richard threateningly. “There is no turning back, do you understand?”

Richard feels a chill down his spine when he looks back into Gareth’s lifeless eyes.

TWO

Gareth drives down the suburban road slowly, with the top of his car down. Richard follows a few cars behind in a nondescript white panel van. The windows of the panel van have been tinted; it is the only distinguishing factor.

He watches the girl as she walks across the road at the pedestrian crossing, and he is immediately interested in her. The dimple in Gareth's cheek deepens as he smiles pleased.

Gareth slows down when he reaches her. He leans his one elbow across the door of his wine-red Mercedes, and he gives her his most seductive smile. Girls usually like him. He is rich, his hair is blond, his eyes are blue, and he

is every girl's dream boyfriend.

He says, friendly, "Hi."

She looks across her shoulder suspiciously, but Gareth sees her defences drop away when she notices him. She smiles prettily and replies, "Hi." She stops walking.

He stops the car along the curb and gets out. After he closes the door, he leans against it, half sitting on it. He says invitingly, "I have to do this social project to determine what makes the perfect teen, and I was wondering if you would mind taking part." He sees her hesitate, so he adds quickly, "We can do it right here." There is no reason why she would not trust him. He is only two or three years older than her; he is well dressed, and he can see from the expression on her face that she does not perceive him to be a threat.

She smiles shyly and her hand comes up timidly to touch her tousled shoulder-length brown hair.

He asks expectantly, smiling invitingly, "So, can I get my camera?"

She giggles nervously. "I suppose it will be okay."

He smiles as he pretends to be relieved. "Thank you. You are a lifesaver." From the corner of his eye, he sees

the panel van parked a short distance ahead of his car. He walks away from the girl toward the back of his car and she turns to look at him. Her back is turned to the panel van.

From the trunk of his car, he gets his expensive video camera and then as he focuses the lens on her, he switches it to record.

Embarrassed she laughs. “What am I supposed to say?”

“Tell me your name.”

“Sarah. Sarah O’Neil.”

“How old are you Sarah?”

“Sixteen.”

“Where do you go to school?”

She looks across the road at a passing car. “I go to school at G.W. High School.”

“Tell me about your hobbies.”

“This is silly.” She giggles again.

He laughs with her. “Okay, then just tell me what makes you the perfect teen.”

“I wouldn’t say I am the perfect teen, but I like to think I am pretty close to being perfect.”

"Are you a cheerleader?"

Sarah blushes. "Yes, actually cheer captain."

Gareth cannot believe his luck. "So, tell me about yourself, it doesn't have to be anything personal, it is just for this stupid project I have to do for my Social Economics class."

"Okay." She smiles again. "I love to party, and I like to listen to music. I don't really have a favourite band, but I like anything on the top forty charts. I am doing well at school and there is no doubt that I will be homecoming queen this year." She stops talking embarrassed as a flush spread across her cheeks.

Gareth looks away from the camera and directly at her. "Is that it, Sarah? If you had to say one thing to describe you, to make people like you, what would it be?"

She says without hesitation, "I am pretty."

He lowers the camera and switches the recording button off.

Smiling at her friendly, he says, "Thank you, Sarah. You were terrific."

Gareth glances past her at Richard and nods his head unnoticeable. This is Richard's signal and he runs forward

from the point where he was standing a few feet behind Sarah, just out of view of the camera. He pulls the black cloth over her face quickly and before she can yell or fight, Gareth grabs her legs. They lift her squirming body and then push her into the back of the panel van roughly. From the moment Gareth lowered the camera and said thank you to her, it took only fifty-seven seconds to grab her and to get her into the back of the van. They can hear her flailing around in the back of the van, but Gareth had painstakingly made the entire back area of the van soundproof. She can yell to her heart's content, but no-one will hear her while she is in the back of the van.

Delightedly Gareth gives Richard a high-five. "Well done, that was not bad for your first kidnapping. I say, we are born to do this."

Richard laughs loudly and then turns away from Gareth. "I'll see at the lodge."

"I'll be right behind you."

As they drive out of the city, Richard increases the volume on the car stereo so that he is unable to hear the banging coming from the interior of the van behind him.

When they arrive at the lodge, they drive up the dusty,

unpaved lane to the wooden shack hidden behind a curtain of large, dense leaved trees.

They stop behind each other and then they both approach the back of the van cautiously. Richard stands ready to stop Sarah should she decide to make a run for it.

Gareth unlocks the back doors and as they swing open, Sarah lunges at him. He punches his fist and hits her straight in the face. His knuckles connect with her eye socket and with a gasp she falls back onto her back.

Sarah feels the pain shoot through to the back of her head and she feels dazed.

Gareth shakes his painful hand next to his side and he exclaims, "Bitch!" He grabs her by her leg and he pulls her out of the van. Her head bangs loudly, agonizingly against the fender and then mercifully she blacks out.

Richard, who is built sturdier than Gareth, picks her up off the ground and hurls her over his shoulder roughly.

Gareth looks around nervously, although he knows there is nobody within miles who could witness what they are doing. He follows Richard to the cabin, and then he squeezes past him to unlock and open the door.

The door swings open and a waft of stale air floats out

through the door.

Gareth pulls his nose up in disgust as he mumbles, "Would think after the last two weekends this place has had enough air."

In silence, Richard carries the unconscious Sarah across the room, past the stone fireplace and then down the stairs to the basement.

In the basement, he and Gareth have constructed six cubicles with drywall over the last two weekends. Although the previous weekend, every aspect of the manual labour was left to Richard to complete, because Gareth was setting up the elaborate electronic equipment, which they have positioned in the lounge area of the cabin.

When Richard walks into the basement, he looks around pleased. He is thrilled with his handy work, and even if he has to say it to himself, he did a good job.

There are no doors on the cubicles, but he put the drywalls up in a way that their captives will be unable to look at each other across the small passageway which runs through the middle. There are three narrow cubicles along each side of the dark, dank basement.

Unceremoniously he drops Sarah onto the cold cement

floor of the first cubicle. She lands with a thud and it is with satisfaction that he hears her head bang against the floor. He pulls her by her arm and then he cuffs her wrist to the metal ring he plastered into the concrete floor.

She is still knocked out, so he fills the plastic dog bowl with water from a big container in the laundry area, and then he places it on the floor near her head.

Silently, he turns away from her still body and he walks back up the creaky wooden stairs to the lounge, where Gareth is waiting for him.

Gareth is sitting in front of the large screen, between large, humming boxes and cables lying haphazardly all over the desk. He is uploading the video he took earlier of Sarah and working on creating a unique logo for their online reality show.

Richard stands behind him silently and he watches Gareth work his magic with the computer. He is impressed, but after ten minutes he becomes bored, so he turns away and walks toward the kitchen area. He opens the fridge and bends into it to pull out two cans of beer. He pulls the tab off the one and then he takes a long swallow. He smiles disturbingly as he considers what hard

work kidnapping is. It takes a lot of pre-planning and physical exertion.

Distracted, he puts the empty beer can on the counter next to him, as he leans with his back against the cupboard behind him and he opens the second can of beer. He sips the beer from the second can slowly as he looks out the window at the back garden of the small log cabin. The trees are gathered closely together, and he watches as the shadows grow higher and higher.

He stands mesmerized as he stares out of the window, his mind blank. When Gareth suddenly speaks behind him, he jumps in his skin. "All done, we can go."

Richard moves away from the counter. "One down, five to go."

THREE

The next day, Gareth invites Samantha to go with him to the movies that night.

At first, she hesitates and makes a feeble excuse of having to study for the end of semester exams, but Gareth knows she has a crush on him. There are not a lot of girls in this world who are immune to his charms.

He smiles charmingly. "Come on, Sammy. The movie is what, two hours long at the most. I promise I'll have you back at ten, at the latest."

She smiles up at him, unsure. He leans down and places his palms on each side of her, holding firmly onto the armrests of her wheelchair. He leans closer to her and he

lets his eyes linger on hers. He sees the moment she considers the possibility that he might like her.

Gareth smiles slowly when Samantha agrees, and he straightens up again.

For the past seven days, they have carefully hand-picked their victims, except for Sarah, who they kidnapped the day before at the spur of the moment. The girl they had been watching and who was a prime candidate escaped unknowing that she was ever in any danger. Her happy life will carry on and never will she know how close she was to experience fear beyond her wildest nightmares.

Gareth was impressed with Richard and the way he totally embraced the role of a stalker. Gareth suggested to Richard how and where they should find their victims, and although he always made it seem as if it was a joint decision, Gareth knew that everything they have done so far was his sole decision and the careful exploitation of Richard.

That evening Gareth collects Samantha in front of the entrance to her dorm, in his expensive wine-red Mercedes.

Smiling seductively as he looks at her suggestively, he lifts her from her wheelchair and gently he places her in

the front passenger seat of his car. After he folds the wheelchair, he puts it into the trunk of his car.

They talk pleasantly about school and exams as they drive toward the mall. When they arrive and after he parks his car in the underground parking area, he helps her out of the car again.

As he walks next to her, and she chats up to him excitedly, he thinks irritated how they must walk across the entire mall to get to the lifts, when they have walked past two escalators already.

They eventually reach the top floor where the cinema is located.

Samantha waits for him while he goes to the refreshment counter and he buys a container of popcorn and a large fizzy drink. As he walks back to her, he pops open the plastic covering of the cold drink container with his thumb and the side his pinkie. He lifts the lid only a fraction, and then he drops the two pills in the palm of his hand into the drink. He does not have to crush it because she is not going to look inside, and the fizzy drink will make the drug dissolve faster. Also, she will be drinking it through a straw, so it is not as if her lips or tongue will

suddenly encounter a solid, foreign object.

When he reaches her, he smiles sexily and then he hands her the popcorn while he quickly pushes the plastic covering on the drink into place tightly.

He asks, "Would you mind holding the drink as well while I push you up the ramp?"

"Of course." She holds her hand up to him and she takes the drink from him.

He smiles, friendly. "I thought we could share." He pretends to be shocked at his own presumptions that she would want to share with him. He apologizes quickly, "I am sorry, I wasn't thinking. I shouldn't just have presumed you would want to share with me."

He sees the pleased look on her face and successfully he hides his deep inner revulsion when she says, "I don't mind." As if to prove her point, she takes a long satisfying drink from the straw.

Gareth smiles, pleased.

He looks around the almost empty area. He chose this day because the movies are usually quieter, and he knew there would not be a lot of people around. The few people walking past them does not even give them a second look.

Gareth sits down on the low wall of the disabled ramp, and he and Samantha are face to face, level with each other. "Shall we wait here for a bit? I do not like it when I must sit inside the theatre and wait for the movie to start. There are too many paper crumpling noises, and you can hear the people behind you are eating. It really works on my nerves."

"I don't mind. We can talk a little."

They talk about school and as they talk, Samantha takes sip after sip of the drink.

Ten minutes later, just as he would have had no choice to push her into the movie theatre, he sees her eyelids droop. He did not want to push her into the movie theatre because to get her out again with her wheelchair, while she was fast asleep, would have attracted too much attention to him.

After a few more minutes, he stands up from the low wall he is sitting on. He steps behind her and then he pushes her back through the mall. When he walks into the lift, there is an elderly woman already in there. He realizes it will look too suspicious for him to back out again.

The old lady looks down at Samantha sympathetic.

Begrudgingly Gareth explains, “She’s had a long day.”

The old woman smiles at him. “You are a good young man to look after her so nicely.”

Gareth just smiles charmingly.

When he gets to his car, Gareth picks her up out of the wheelchair and gently he sits her down onto the seat. He buckles the safety belt around her, and he lets the seat down a bit so that her head does not drop forward awkwardly. He folds up her wheelchair again and then he places it in the trunk of his car.

He drives away from the mall slowly, aware of the multitude of security cameras adorning the wall.

At the university grounds, he drives his car through the parking area in front of her dorm and then slowly he drives around to the back.

He turns down a little service road behind her dorm, protected by large trees on either side until he sees the panel van ahead of him.

Moments later, he stops in front of the van, the headlights of his Mercedes illuminates Richard in the front seat of the white panel van.

Richard jumps out and walks to the back of the van.

As Gareth gets out of his car, he hears the back doors of the van swing open. He lifts Samantha up from the chair roughly with a grunt. She is heavy and deeply sedated from the sleeping tablets Richard stole from his mother's large supply.

He struggles as he carries her toward the back of the van and then relieved, he drops her down onto the metal floor of the van with a bang.

Richard smiles. "With her you can tick off both black and disabled."

Gareth smirks sarcastically. "Will you get her to the cabin? I have to go to the library now, to tighten my alibi."

"All sorted. I'll be back in a little over an hour."

"I'll see you back in the room." Still trying to catch his breath, Gareth gets back into his car.

Richard drives casually away from the university grounds. He waves friendly to the guard at the entrance gates and then as he reaches the straight, smooth tarmac of the highway, he turns the volume on the stereo louder. He sings with the songs he knows and taps the beat of the music on the steering wheel with the tips of his fingers.

When he reaches the shack, he carries the unconscious

Samantha slung across his broad shoulder into the structure.

He cannot wait for the day when the video goes live, and he will at last be an internet sensation. They have chosen the screen name of The Death Factor. Gareth created a fake email account with false information and connected the video channel to this phony email account. Richard has never really been much use in front of a computer. He knows how to do the basic things like post his status, do projects on his word documents and to upload photos and videos to the internet, and he does not really know what all the gadgets surrounding the computer in the lounge is for, but it looks impressive and Gareth is the ultimate computer genius.

In the basement, he shackles Samantha to the metal ring in the cubicle next to Sarah.

As he fills her dog bowl with water and fills the other bowl with dog kibble, he hears Sarah mumble.

Frowning displeased, he walks into Sarah's cubicle and notices she is still asleep. He picks up the dog food bowl and walks back to the counter by the washing machine. He refills her bowl with water and fills another with kibble. A

hungry stomach does not care what it gets to eat, besides, they chose a top of the range dog food, and all their contestants will have a well-balanced, nutritional meal every day. Softly he laughs cynically at his own cleverness and then he hears Sarah scream at the top of her lungs. "Help! Help me!"

He storms back to her with the bowl of water still in his hand. He hurls the bowl directly into her face. The water sprays in an arc across the wall behind her.

"Shut up, bitch! Stop screaming, nobody can hear you out here. Save your breath for when you have to plead for your life," he screams close to her face. He sees his spit spew over her face, and she grimaces.

Her hand comes up to grab at him, but he sidesteps deftly and as she comes up onto her knees to crawl after him, he steps further away. She rushes toward him, and then when she reaches the end of her chain, it jerks her back. She lands onto the floor with a loud dull sound.

"When you get thirsty you can lick the water off the wall behind you, stupid bitch."

He takes the red plastic bowl, which he filled earlier with kibble and slides it across the floor. It stops close to

her foot and she kicks at it. Kibble flies everywhere.

Richard smirks as he turns around away from her. "Now you can eat your food from off the ground as well."

He mumbles to himself as he walks up the stairs and out to his car to get Samantha's wheelchair. He picks it up out of the back of the van effortlessly and then he carries it into the cabin. He stashes it in the main bedroom.

As he drives away from the dark cabin, he cannot believe how ungrateful that spoilt Sarah is. She should be grateful he comes here every day to feed her and she should be more concerned with keeping herself pretty, so she gets chosen every day to go forward in the competition. If they let her go, she will be in every magazine and on every talk show, and she really should show more gratitude.

FOUR

The police arrive at the campus at lunchtime and when they approach Gareth where he is standing in a group of girls laughing and chatting, he is not surprised to see them.

The police officer flashes his badge at the group and then turns to Gareth. "Mr. Gareth van Rhijn?"

Gareth turns to the officer with a wide, accepting grin on his face. "That's me."

"Can I ask you a few questions?" He takes a notebook from his top shirt pocket and holds the pen ready. He looks back at Gareth questioningly.

"Yeah. What's this about?" He asks friendly.

Seriously the police officer says, "You went out with

Samantha Jones last night. We believe the two of you went to the movies."

Gareth frowns perplexed. "Yes, we did. What's wrong?"

"When was the last time you saw her?"

"I dropped her off last night at about nine, but I cannot remember the exact time. She fell asleep before we even watched the movie, so I brought her home." He shrugs and turns to the girl standing beside him. "Not the most exciting date, if I say so myself."

The girl giggles.

The police officer frowns. "She just fell asleep?"

"Yeah. She did tell me when we were driving there that she is very tired. She only had a few hours' sleep the night before because she was up all night cramming for her Business Economics exam yesterday morning."

The police officer nods his head as he scribbles across the notepad.

Gareth knows where the security cameras are on the university grounds and he also knows that the one which monitors the entrance to Samantha's dorm has not been working for the last two months. Nobody will ever know

he drove past her dorm and that he did not drop her off where he was supposed to. Also, Samantha had a single dorm room. She needed the extra space for her wheelchair, so he would not have to explain why nobody heard his car when he supposedly dropped her off in front of the dorm.

"After you dropped Samantha off, where did you go?"

"She woke up just as we stopped in front of her dorm, and she did not want to invite me in." He glances at the girl standing next to him again, with an amused grin on his face.

The police officer clears his throat irritated. "What did you do thereafter, Mr. van Rhijn?"

"I went to the library and I stayed there until eleven when they closed up shop. What's going on anyway? Why are you asking me these questions, did something happen to Samantha?"

The police officer turns away from Gareth. "It is an ongoing investigation; so please remain available in case I have more questions for you."

"Of course, Officer," Gareth replies obligingly.

When the police officer walks away from their group,

Gareth turns to the girls surrounding him. He asks nobody in particular, and there is a tone of concern in his voice. "I wonder what's going on."

That night Gareth gets dressed leisurely. He pulls on a charcoal coloured pair of designer jeans and he buttons up the mauve and white striped dress shirt.

He glances across the room at Richard, who is sitting in front of his desk pouring over his Advanced Engineering Manual. "Remember to come by Claire's house at eleven."

"I'll be there," Richard replies distractedly. Being an internet sensation is not going to give him a degree in Chemical Engineering, so even with the most exciting thing happening in his life, he still has to pass his exams.

Ten minutes later Gareth leaves their dorm room and with a confident swagger in his every step he walks to his car.

He drives away from the university grounds and out to the gated secure estate not far from the university. Claire invited him this morning to a house party at her house, which is a pure good coincidence. They have been

monitoring her brother since they had decided to proceed with this venture of theirs. And now it seems providence is indeed on their side.

He arrives at the large, palatial house and he parks his car in the road behind another car. Walking up to the impressive house, he surveys the affluent neighbourhood, which he has been in many times before, interested. As part of Claire's park like garden, there is an open field with large oak trees to the side, and he and Richard decided earlier this is where Gareth will leave Claire's brother to be collected.

Gareth knocks the elegant brass knocker against the hand carved wooden door, and after a few minutes Claire opens the door. Her eyes light up excited when she sees him.

He leans into her and brushes his warm lips against her cheek softly, making her think he is romantically interested in her.

They walk into the house and into a room filled with young bodies. He stays close to her side and he keeps his arm draped across her shoulder, making her believe she is the only girl in the room he could ever be interested in.

An hour later, he asks her, "Is it okay if I use your house phone. I'll only be two seconds." He smiles down at her enchantingly. "I forgot to charge my phone this afternoon."

She nods her head and then she walks with him to the phone installed against the wall in the kitchen. "There you go. I am going to powder my nose."

He leans closer into her and then he says softly, charmingly, "I'll miss you."

She walks away smiling across her shoulder at him alluringly and he picks up the receiver. When he sees Claire leave the room, he turns his back on the people gathered in the kitchen.

He phones the security office at the entrance gates to the secure estate.

When they answer, he says in a gruff voice, "Hi. I am phoning from the Peterson residence."

"Yes, sir. May I help you?"

"We forgot to add a name to our list of guests. Can I give it to you now?"

Uncertainly the guard says, "Okay."

Gareth hears a ruffle of papers, and then the guard

asks, "The name of your guest?"

"Richard Smith. He should be arriving at about eleven-ish."

"Okay, Mr. Peterson."

"Sorry for only phoning you with an extra name now, I know it goes against the rules, but I will be grateful for this one lapse."

The guard laughs nervously. He is new, but he has been told Mr. Peterson is not an easy man to please and he often yells and screams at the guards when they are not fast enough to let him in or out of the estate. The guard only assumes he is talking to Mr. Peterson because the music in the background is loud and the voice is muffled.

Gareth says, "Thank you, George." He read the name from his name tag earlier in the evening when he came in.

Before George can say anything, Gareth ends the call.

As he puts the phone back in the cradle, he hears Claire's voice as she comes walking into the kitchen.

She looks up at him infatuated. "All done?"

He walks to her and kisses her lightly on the cheek. "Thank you so much. I owe you one."

They dance a few dances and it is getting late. Gareth

is starting to feel panicked because he cannot see Alex, Claire's brother, anywhere in the room.

He leans into Claire. "Let's go outside to get some fresh air."

She smiles up at him without saying a word and then leading him by the hand, she guides him through the throng of people out to the back-patio doors.

Alex is sitting sprawled on a deckchair next to the swimming pool. There is a bored expression on his face.

Gareth greets him friendly. "Hey. Claire tells me you had a very good game again last weekend."

Alex perks up and sitting up straight on the deckchair, he smiles brightly.

Alex and Gareth start to talk about football and a few minutes later, Claire exclaims, "A good party for me, means no football talk. I am going inside."

Gareth slides his arm around her waist and pulls her into him. He brings his head down to her and he whispers suggestively in her ear. "I'll come and find you soon." He pulls away from her slowly and smiles down at her as he captures her gaze with his.

She smiles up at him. If it was not that he had more

important things to consider, he could have gotten lucky tonight. He considers though that after he disposes of his immediate and most important task of the evening, he could always go and find her. He could imagine a few things he would want to do with her, and she looked as if she was more than willing to oblige him his every whim.

After Claire disappears into the house, Gareth turns to Alex. "You want something to drink?"

"Unless you are offering me a beer, then no."

Gareth smiles, friendly. "And if I said, I could offer you something stronger than beer, what would you say?"

"I'd say bring it on."

Gareth sits down on the deck chair next to Alex. He puts his legs up and leans his back against the inclined backrest, as he pulls the bottle from his jacket pocket and he twists off the silver lid. He pretends to have a drink from the open bottle and then he hands it over to Alex.

Alex takes a deep swallow and then hands the bottle back.

They start talking about football again and obviously the young man loves his sport. He is a jock, full of his high school self-importance and he does not mind talking

about himself.

Without taking a sip, Gareth passes the bottle back to Alex.

Soon Alex starts to laugh at nothing, and his eyes start to glaze over. He stands up and he wobbles on his feet for a moment.

Gareth jumps up and holds onto him to steady him. "Whoa, Alex."

Alex slurs, "My mom is going to kill me when she sees me like this. How much of that bottle did we drink?"

Gareth lifts the bottle to eye-level and sees Alex has drunk a little more than half the large bottle of Vodka all by himself.

"Do you want to sleep it off in my car? I am only leaving after everybody is gone."

Alex nods his head and gags. For a moment Gareth fears Alex is going to puke on him and smelling of puke will ruin his alibi.

"Is there a back way out of here?" Gareth asks as he glances around the back garden purposefully.

Wildly Alex points to the side of the house.

Gareth squints his eyes, trying to see through the dark

shadows in the direction of Alex's wavering, pointing finger.

Relieved Gareth sees the side gate and is also immediately thankful it is on the same side as the open park-like field. He most certainly does not want to risk anybody seeing him helping the drunken Alex across the brightly lit lawn in front of the house.

With Alex hanging from him, Gareth carries, drags him out the side gate. He stops to look if the way is clear, and he sees the shrubs are high. This side of the house is shrouded in darkness. Slowly he helps Alex to the side of the house and then into the field.

Alex asks garbled, "Where we going?"

Patiently Gareth explains, "To my car. Almost there."

When they reach an oak tree, Gareth lets Alex sit, propped up by the trunk of the oak tree. "Sit here for a bit, I'll bring my car closer."

As Gareth steps away, he lifts his forearm and looks at the time on his watch. Excellent timing. He walks away from the tree and as he walks unnoticed through the side gate into Claire's back garden, he looks back and sees Richard's Jeep pull up next to the sidewalk.

They decided it would be better for Richard to bring his own car, rather than the panel van. People will remember seeing a panel van in this upper-class suburban area, but every second youngster has a Jeep, so nobody will remember it as something out of place.

Quietly Gareth walks around the house and then goes back inside through the patio doors, looking for Claire.

Richard lifts the drunken boy from the ground easily. Alex mumbles a few incoherent words, but Richard ignores him as he lays him down onto the back seat of his Jeep. He throws a pile of blankets over him while Alex complains incoherently.

He drives out through the open gate, smiling friendly at the security guard and then he drives out to the cabin in the woods.

After an hour, he reaches the dark structure. It is almost invisible in the dark, with the shadows of the trees surrounding it.

He leaves his headlights on so he can see what he is doing. He opens the back door and pulls Alex by his legs until he can grip him around his waist.

Alex is passed out and a dead weight. With a heave,

Richard manages to get Alex over his shoulder and then he carries him into the cabin.

He pushes his shoulder against the light switch just inside the door, and the fluorescent light flickers on brightly.

The light shines halfway down the stairs, and the rest of the way Richard feels his way, stepping carefully so he does not lose his footing and stumble, headfirst, down the stairs.

He follows his instincts in the dark room and then he puts Alex in an empty cubicle. Quickly he cuffs Alex to the metal ring in the floor. Alex gives a long, loud snore and amused Richard considers that tomorrow the boy will wake up with a terrible thirst and an immense headache.

Feeling his way to the laundry area, he switches on the soft, amber light.

He walks back to the other two cubicles to fetch the food and water bowls.

They are both fast asleep. Gareth suggested they grind sleeping pills and add it to their water.

It won't do if they hurt themselves—who would vote for them then?

When Richard looks down at the pretty sleeping face of Sarah, he notices the blotches of blood on her cheeks. He scrutinizes her a little more carefully and he sees her nails on the unshackled hand are broken down into her flesh, and her fingers are covered in dried blood. He shakes his head sadly as he backs away from her, and once again he cannot believe how selfish and ungrateful, she is.

In the cubicle next door, he notices Samantha has hauled herself upright against the drywall. Her legs are spread out on the floor at an odd angle and her head rests uncomfortably on her shoulder.

He smirks as he considers her to be an idiot. Honestly, why would a person sleep in such an uncomfortable position? In the yellow glow of the faint low wattage bulb, he sees shadows of tear tracks down her cheeks.

Without any emotion, he gets the dog bowls and then he fills them.

His first stepfather slapped the crap and emotion out of him years ago, and frankly, Richard had none left to share.

He places a water bowl and a food bowl, filled with dog food, in each cubicle.

Methodically, he retraces his steps, as he switches off the light before he takes the stairs to the top floor.

As he drives away from the blackened cottage back to the dorm, he worries about the test he must write in the morning. Maybe he can study for another hour or two before he hits the sack.

FIVE

'*Bad to the bone*', Gareth's ringtone echoes through the kiddies play area, where he is sitting next to the Spanish nanny, who is the caretaker for the cute, little eight-year-old Emily.

Emily has big blue eyes and her hair is tied up in two pigtails on the sides of her face. Gareth knows she will go far in the competition to be the one and only survivor of his online reality show.

Gareth answers the phone after he smiles apologetically to Maria. He has been meeting her here every afternoon between three and four. "Yes."

Richard asks, "So is everything ready for me to collect

the package this afternoon?"

"It is. Be there at ten to four." Gareth ends the call.

He sighs melodramatically as he looks back at Maria. "My mom. I have to go and help her move some boxes this afternoon."

Maria smiles up at him. She could not believe her luck that this handsome young man, the same age as her, has taken an interest in her. She is here in America, far away from home, and he is the first person who started speaking to her as if she was a human being and not just an employee. The way he looks at her, makes her feel special and he has nagged her since the second day he met her here on the bench on the verge of the kiddie play area to go out with him. She has declined shyly each time, but if he asked her today, she would say yes because tonight it is her night off.

Gareth laughs and jokes with Maria, and he knows the effect he has on her. He can see the little signs she is sending him, like the way she averts her eyes shyly every now and again, the way her cheeks flush pink every so often. He would have enjoyed having a brief romantic liaison with her, but he had to concentrate on the bigger

picture. They are halfway there. They have three kids, and there is only three more to go. If they can kidnap Emily successfully today, there will only be two left to go and the last two will be the easiest. They have set a goal, and next week the online video must be uploaded to their video channel of choice.

At a quarter to four, Gareth says to Maria, "If I give you money, why don't you go to that ice-cream vendor there and buy all three of us an ice-cream?"

Maria glances at Emily where she is sliding down the slide. "I can't."

Gareth smiles enigmatically. "I'll keep an eye on Emily. Besides, you'll be just over there, and you will still be able to see her."

"I suppose it will be okay."

Gareth lifts himself a little from the bench as he reaches into his pocket to pull a few notes from his wallet. "Buy us the most expensive ones there are."

She takes the money shyly and then she gets up from the bench. She glances at Emily and then before she walks away, she asks Gareth, "What flavour do you prefer, Chris?" Yes, he lied to her. He did not give her his real

name, because although this is another jurisdiction from the police officer who questioned him the other day regarding the disappearance of Samantha, you never know when there will be an overeager detective putting two and two together. It will not help if his name keeps cropping up every time a young person is stolen. He is not worried if she will be able to describe him to the police because he looks astoundingly just like every other typical American youngster—blond hair, blue eyes, perfect features, fashionably dressed.

Maria walks away and for a moment he enjoys watching the sway of her hips. He looks away from her annoyed with himself, and then he pushes himself up from off the bench. He chose today specifically. He has been coming here for two weeks, since the night they agreed and decided to put his idea into motion. He knows today it is the quietest day of the whole week. There is a group of nannies on the other side of the park, but they are huddled together gossiping and laughing amongst themselves.

He walks into the fenced area, directly to Emily. When he gets to her, he smiles down at her kindly. "Do you want

an ice-cream?"

She does not yell stranger-danger because she has seen him every day for two weeks, excluding Sunday. He has talked to her every day and now, unfortunately for her, she trusts him.

She jumps up with glee. "Yes."

"Then come with me, little one."

She takes his hand and her tiny hand disappears into his. It is warm and grainy with sand from the sandpit.

He walks with her out of the fenced area and then they walk back to the bench.

Gareth sees Richard waiting there for them. Richard is standing in the shadows of the trees around the perimeter of the park area. When Gareth and Emily approach the bench, Richard steps out from between the trees.

Gareth goes down on his one knee in front of Emily, after he glances across his shoulder quickly. Maria has her back turned to him, and she is bending over double as she rummages through the ice-cream icebox.

Gareth smiles widely. "My friend says he will take you to get an ice-cream while I stay here and wait for Maria. When Maria comes back, I'll tell her and then we will come

and get you."

Emily shakes her head in denial. "I don't know your friend. I can only go with you. Maria and my Mommy will be angry with me, if I go with somebody I don't know."

Gareth struggles to continue smiling, as he straightens himself out. He takes Emily's hand in his again and then he says, friendly, "Very clever, Emily. I am proud of you for not leaving with a stranger. I think you deserve a double scoop. What flavour do you like? My favourite is chocolate chip."

Emily skips playfully next to Gareth as they walk away from the play area. "I love strawberry and chocolate ice-cream."

Five minutes later, Maria's panicked scream echoes from a distance toward them.

Richard scoops Emily up into his arms and he walks as fast as he can with the child in his arms to the panel van. Emily cries out loudly, and although there are people looking at Richard suspiciously, nobody stops him.

Gareth turns away and shakes his head in disgust when an overweight woman stops to look back at Richard hurrying away. He says with loathing, "Some fathers are

really terrible at looking after their kids. The poor child was probably having fun at the park, and now she doesn't want to leave."

The heavyset woman looks back at Gareth and he can see her accept this as the only possible explanation.

Richards buckles Emily into the front seat of the panel van as Emily continues screaming at the top of her lungs. Obviously, he cannot shove her into the back of the panel van, there are too many witnesses.

A man and a woman walk past and Richard smiles across his shoulder at them with a flustered look. He turns back to Emily and he says admonishingly, "Emily. Stop that now, we must get home. You have been at the park all day."

Hopefully, Emily looks up at him. She stops screaming as she asks expectantly, "Are we going home?"

The lady standing on the sidewalk smiles sympathetically and then both the man and woman continue walking away.

Richard hisses, close to Emily's face. "You see, nobody cares about you, so shut the fuck up."

Defeated Emily slumps back into the seat and then

tears start running down her cheeks as she softly moans, "I want my Mommy."

Her crying is starting to work on his nerves and after twenty minutes of continuous crying and moaning, he yells annoyed, "If you don't shut up now, I am going to hit you so hard, you will have a fucking reason to cry."

Emily glances up at him sideways, but she starts crying even louder, as fear fills her little body.

He hits his palm against the side of her head violently, and her head thuds against the side of the door on her side loudly.

Emily huddles away from him and continues to whimper softly.

Richard increases the volume on the car stereo, and he drowns out her quiet snivelling.

When they arrive at the cabin, it is still light out.

He walks around the van and then he pulls Emily roughly from the passenger seat.

Holding her horizontally in his one arm, he carries her to the wood structure. He unlocks the door and immediately he notices the stink of human excrement. It fills the air and cloys annoyingly in his nose. He makes a

mental note to discuss the toilet facilities with Gareth. Someone is going to have to clean all that shit from the floors and from the kids and it is not going to be him.

Emily kicks violently, squirming to get out of his arm. She screams loudly.

Richard holds onto her tightly as he starts to laugh agitated while he carries her down into the basement. The basement is dark because there is not a single window down here.

He switches on the faint light, and then he takes Emily to her cubicle. He shackles her to the metal ring on the floor and she begs, "I want my Mommy. Please get me my Mommy."

Richard ignores her.

Systematically he fills the food bowls. He fills the water bowls from the five-litre container with the magic sleeping potion. While he works, he remembers the time he volunteered at the animal shelter during a summer holiday a long time ago, and this feels the same.

Alex looks dead, so he kicks him hard with the tip of his shoe in the ribs. Alex groans.

Sarah's wrist is raw, blood caked grossly around her

arm like a grotesque bangle, and Samantha is still in the same position as the day before.

The sedative they are giving them is strong, maybe too strong, but it keeps them quiet and next week they will lessen the dosage, they cannot have zombie looking kids on the video footage. The world must choose the typical teen and surely drugged out and dopey looking will not do the trick of turning Richard into an overnight anonymous internet sensation.

The crying child is irritating him, so before he does something he will regret, he walks away to go back to the city.

As he switches off the light and everything becomes black, Emily screams in terror, "No! Please leave the light on. I am scared of the dark and I promise I'll be good. Please!"

He walks up the stairs and then after he locks the door securely, he drives away.

SIX

Gareth and Richard sit in the panel van. The inside of the van is dark, and Richard has parked the vehicle in between two lampposts so only a faint amber glow is shining onto the car. The kid across the street might become suspicious when he sees two white young men sitting in a car staring and watching him absorbed.

Richard has followed the fourteen-year-old, black youth around for a few days. He has learned the kid stays on the corner until four o'clock each morning, catching the early morning stragglers as they leave the nightclubs and looking for a fix or to replenish their stock. Each morning at four o'clock the kid then goes home to a filthy

Brownstone house. Black bags of rubbish are piled on the steps and some are spilling over onto the sidewalk. One morning when Richard did not have to rush off to get in a few hours of sleep before heading to class, he saw the fourteen-year-old boy leave the disgusting squalor with a ten-year-old girl. Although the girl did not have any physical injuries, she had the haunted look of an abused child. Interested he followed the children around the block and then he saw the young boy buy the little girl a burger and drink before he walked with her across the road and down four blocks. At the school, he went down on his one knee in front of the girl and Richard instinctively knew that the little girl is the young boy's sister.

For a moment, he considered to rather kidnap the girl, but then he remembered they were looking for the perfect kid, not the sorriest looking kid.

Tonight, they have been watching the boy wordlessly for more than an hour, and it is almost four o'clock. The road is dark and deserted, all the street vermin have crawled into their respective holes.

Richard jumps with fright when he hears the passenger

side door open. Silently, he watches Gareth get out of the car, and he follows him with his eyes as Gareth crosses the road in front of the van.

Gareth approaches the boy with a confident swagger. “Hey.”

The young boy looks up at Gareth nervously.

Gareth says friendly, “I hear you are the man to see if I need something.”

The boy looks up and down the road apprehensively. He cannot afford to be arrested. He cannot leave his sister alone with their sadistic father and pathetic mother.

Gareth takes out his wallet and then he pulls a hundred-dollar bill from the fold. “I hear you are cheap.”

The boy remains standing with his back against the wall, looking up at Gareth searchingly.

“You can keep the change.”

The boy looks at the hundred-dollar bill, flapping in the slight early morning breeze. He reaches his hand into his pocket to pull out the little packet of drugs. His mind works fast. Julio, his boss, will not know he got paid a hundred dollars for a twenty-dollar sachet. He would be able to take eighty dollars’ home and this afternoon he can

spoil Anna. He loved seeing her happy smile when it appeared now and again, and sadly it did not happen often enough.

He holds the sachet to Gareth while his other hand reaches up to the money.

Gareth grabs hold of the boy's skinny, emaciated wrist and then he pulls him roughly to him. Richard is next to him in seconds because he knows Gareth is not big and strong enough to do the physical labour.

Richard grabs the boy from behind, around the waist and then he carries him to the panel van. The boy screams, but there is nobody to hear him, the industrial area is desolate at this hour. He kicks violently and his foot hits Richard in the groin.

Richard yells out in pain. "Fuck, kid." He punches the boy against the back of the head hard and the sound is dull but effective. The boy slumps down in his arms, and annoyed Richard hurls the boy into the back of the panel van. The child's body bounces off the side, and then slumps down into a sorry heap.

Richard rubs his groin, trying to get the sharp excruciating pain to subside.

He walks to the front of the van and he slides into the driver seat, with a painful groan. Gareth is already waiting for him.

"Do you want me to drive out to the cabin with you?"

Richard suggests, "While we got this one, why don't we just drive two blocks on and get that other kid. He sleeps under the bridge."

With a frown, Gareth asks, "What about the other homeless people? Won't they try to stop us?"

"No. I have discovered in the last few days following him around that homeless people are very territorial, and he sleeps there with only four or five other kids. This would be a good time because it is still dark, so when I grab him from under the bridge, the other kids there won't be able to see my face too clearly."

As Richard starts the van, he pulls the car into the road, driving toward the bridge, Gareth agrees. "Okay. We might as well get this over and done with. You'll have to drop me off though before you drive to the cabin, I have an eleven o'clock class, I cannot miss. Are you free today?"

"I have a class this afternoon at four, so hopefully I'll be able to get a few hours of sleep in before then. At least

it is Saturday tomorrow."

Gareth suggests, "We can upload the first video tomorrow, or do you have any other plans?"

"None."

"Good. So, we upload the video tomorrow, and then by next week Thursday, we can have the final climatic episode. Perfect timing, in my opinion, cause my parents expect me home for Thanksgiving dinner."

As they approach the bridge, they stop talking about their normal, daily activities. Richard switches off the engine of the car, and he lets the van roll down the slight incline, closer to the bridge. He does not want to carry a writhing and kicking kid up to the main road. His groin is still shooting sharp pains down his legs.

Richard stops the car and then without hesitation, he opens the door and gets out. With determination, he walks in under the bridge. With the amount of city and streetlights around him, the early morning darkness is not as black as would be expected, so he can see where he is going easily.

He steps across two tiny bodies and he walks directly to the black-haired boy in the corner. He pulls the sleeping

boy up from the ground and then he is surprised when four pair of hands grab onto him.

He throws the nine-year-old, loudly yelling kid across his shoulder and he starts kicking wildly at the four young kids grabbing onto him. He hears the crack of a bone when he kicks a boy of seven in the shin, and the girl rushes off to help him.

Richard bellows in an authoritarian voice, "Unless you want to spend the next few days in jail, step away. This young fellow is wanted for questioning."

The remaining two kids step away from him immediately and the boy in his arms stops thrashing. The kid screams infuriated, "What questioning, I haven't done anything wrong!"

Richard ignores the child and walks out from under the bridge. The two kids who stepped back afraid when they assumed, he was a police officer, run after him. Richard sees Gareth duck under the dashboard in the front of the van. From the corner of his eyes, he sees the one kid's lips move as she tries to memorize the license plate.

He walks around the van and then he pushes the child into the back of the van, after he swings the door open,

preparing to knock the black kid back should he decide to make a run for it.

The black kid is still in the same position he was in when Richard threw him in earlier on.

Richard walks back to the front of the van and then gets in. Gareth is lying down on the seat, and Richard sits with his thigh pressed into the top of his head.

The bright headlights from the van blind the kids standing in front of it, as he switches it on. Their arms fly up to shield their eyes.

Awkwardly, he shifts the gears into reverse, and then eventually he gets the van turned around and he drives up the incline and onto the tarmac.

Gareth sits up and worried he says, "You'll have to get rid of this van."

"I am going to the cabin now and I will stay there. It means I have to skip my class this afternoon, but I suppose I can make a little sacrifice for fame."

"When you get to the cabin, drive it in between the trees. For the rest of the week, we can drive around in your Jeep. Give me your keys and I'll drive up with it tomorrow."

Richard smirks amused. "It was good thinking on your part when we bought this van with my dead father's identification."

"It helped that I paid cash, otherwise they would have made credit checks."

Richard laughs amused. "As if the motor dealer where we bought this van would have even bothered with such technicalities. He saw the cash and everything else disappeared for him."

Gareth laughs with him and thirty minutes later Richard drops him off in front of the dorm.

Still in good humour, Gareth says, "I'll see you tomorrow."

"Bring beer and food."

"Okay. I'll bring enough supplies for the week. How is the dog food, do we need any more?"

"Yeah, buy another big bag."

Gareth smiles widely and then he walks away.

Richard drives away from the university and then he follows the, by now, familiar road out to the cabin.

When he stops in front of the cabin, he sits quietly for a little while, enjoying the hushed tranquillity of his

surroundings.

In the darkened basement, Sarah wakes up groggily. She tries to pull at the metal cuff around her wrist and a sharp ache flashes like a white searing light through her brain. She groans softly in pain and then she hears the soft wailing.

She asks hopefully, her voice hesitant and croaky, “Is there someone there?”

The crying stops abruptly.

Sarah asks again, “Hello?”

Emily sniffs. “I want my Mommy.”

Sarah can hear the youthfulness of the voice. “Where’s your Mommy?”

The little girl starts to sob. “I am scared of the dark. Will you please put the lights on?”

Apologetically Sarah replies, “I can’t. I am tied to the floor.”

The volume of the sobbing increases. Sarah hears a door slam from a distance away.

She implores urgently. “What’s your name?”

Emily hiccups as she tries to swallow her sobs.

"Emily."

"Okay, Emily, listen to me. It is important. Are you listening?"

"Yes."

Sarah can hear a door opening from somewhere above her. "Pretend to be sleeping. Close your eyes. Now."

Emily starts to say, "I can't"

The light above them flicker on and Sarah slumps down onto the cold cement floor.

She keeps her eyes open to slits and she sees the dark shadow walk past. The tall, muscular boy is carrying a child of about nine across his shoulder. With a sickening thud, she hears a body make contact with the floor and then she hears the scraping of metal across the concrete floor. She hears a metal spring jump into place and then the dark figure walks past again. She listens as she hears the footsteps on the stairs leading up and when the door slams shut, she whispers loudly. "Emily? Are you still there?"

The voice is soft. "Yes."

"You were such a good girl. When you hear the footsteps coming down again, you must not say anything. You must be quiet." Sarah waits for a reply. Several

seconds tick by. "Okay?"

Emily whimpers, "But I am scared."

"I know, but you are not alone. You must be brave, and if you are, your Mommy will be proud of you."

Sarah hears the door creak open again and then she hears two pairs of feet coming down the stairs.

Urgently Sarah begs, "Hush. Pretend to be sleeping."

As the dark shadow falls across the wall of her cubicle Sarah suppresses the urge to scream. The boy from earlier is pulling another teenage boy across the room. The boy is thrashing on the floor, but the dog training choke chain is biting into the flesh around his neck and he pulls uselessly onto it with both his hands, the gurgling sound erupting from him is agonizing.

SEVEN

Richard chains the homeless boy onto the floor after kicking him a few times into submission.

Then, feeling accomplished with himself, he walks past the cubicles. It was easier than he would have ever been able to imagine. Six kids neatly stowed away in six cubicles. Now they are ready to start making the video as soon as Gareth arrives in the morning.

He does not feel like feeding them tonight, besides the smell down here will drive him insane. Tomorrow he will lead the drug-selling black kid on the choke chain, and he will have him clean up the place. It stinks.

He goes upstairs and then after he gets a six-pack of

beers from the fridge, he settles himself onto the couch. He pops open the first can as he clicks the button on the remote control. The TV flickers on and after he switches between a few channels, he chooses a movie. He sits back with a beer can in his hand and he stares at the screen mesmerized. Before the movie is finished and the credits starts rolling across the screen, he has sipped his way through all six cans of beer, and he is fast asleep.

Sarah can hear the noise from upstairs and soon she realizes the sounds are from a movie. She asks softly, "Emily?"

"Yes."

"Where are you? Can you see anything around you?"

The child whimpers. "No. It is too dark."

A voice from across Sarah startles her. "It is too dark to see anything. I cannot even see my hand in front of my face."

"Who are you?" Sarah asks bewildered.

"Max."

"Max? How long have you been here?"

"Just arrived. How many of us are here?"

"I don't know."

"How long have you been here?" Max asks, worried.

"I am not sure, and I have been asleep for most of the time—I think anyway. The day I got here, there was a college boy who was asking me questions about being the perfect teen. I honestly thought it was just a joke, but then someone grabbed me from behind and put something over my head. Next thing I knew, we arrived here somewhere in the woods."

Emily cries softly, "I want my Mommy."

Sarah replies to her sad voice, "I promise you I will do everything I can to get us out of here." She pulls her wrist painfully against the metal handcuff again, and despondently she knows she might never fulfil her promise to Emily. She says, "Okay, so we know there is me, Sarah. Also, Emily. Emily, how old are you?"

Emily sobs, "Eight."

Max says, "I am nine."

"Wow, Max. You sound very brave for a nine-year-old." Sarah tries to sound impressed.

"Yeah, well. I have been living on the streets since I have been about seven. You have to learn to be strong

quickly."

"On the streets?" Living in her privileged world, Sarah never even considered the possibility there could be homeless people who are so young.

Max scoffs. "My dad woke up in a bad mood one morning and while calling me a homo, he literally kicked me out of the house. I suppose I could have gone back later after he had a few beers and mellowed out a bit, but after sitting across the house on the side-walk staring back at that house of pain, I decided it could not be any worse if I went somewhere else."

Another voice asks softly from Sarah's left. "What do you think they want to do with us?"

"Who are you?" Max asks harshly.

The soft voice replies, "Samantha."

Sarah asks, worried, "Is there anybody else in here?"

There is a grunt from further back in the darkness and a deep voice says, "Me. Alex."

Max exclaims, "Five so far. It is me, Emily, Samantha, Alex and you, Sarah."

There are a few moments of silence as each of them considers their own predicament, when Max says again,

"No, wait. There are six of us. When they grabbed me and threw me in the back of the van there was another black kid already in the back. He was slumped in the corner and he did not wake up once." He hesitates. "Maybe he is dead already."

Emily wails loudly.

Sarah shushes her, "No, Emily. We must not make a lot of noises. They might hear us."

Emily continues to cry softly.

Samantha asks again, "So what do you think they want with us?"

Alex asks abruptly, "What do we have in common?"

Max replies, "An eight-year-old girl, a nine-year-old boy, the boy with me was black and looked about fourteen—maybe."

Samantha offers, "I am eighteen."

Sarah declares her age, "I am sixteen."

Lastly, Alex contributes his age. "And I am seventeen. So, we are all kids. I heard you say Sarah that the day you were kidnapped, they said they were doing a survey on the perfect teen, so it must have something to do with that. Although being a homeless gay-boy does not really equate

to a perfect teen."

Max exclaims loudly, "Fuck you, asshole."

Sarah gasps shocked, but before she can say something, Samantha adds to the conversation, "I am black, and I am disabled."

Alex laughs derisively. "Also, not the perfect teen."

Sarah inhales loudly. "What is wrong with you? I suppose you consider yourself perfect."

"As a matter of fact, I do. I am popular, rich, football captain, rising star. Also, I am white, perfectly straight, and healthy."

Max calls out disgusted. "You are the worse specimen of a human being I have ever come across."

"Actually. You have not come across me yet, gay-boy. You have only heard me."

They continue arguing and insulting each other right through the night until they hear the door above them creak open and footsteps come down the stairs. The overhead light flickers on.

Shocked Richard looks around when he sees eyes staring up at him in different degrees of emotion. Then he remembers he did not feed them the night before, so they

did not get a dose of the potent sleeping potion. In hindsight, it was probably a good thing he chose not to feed them otherwise they would be all groggy this morning.

He walks past each cubicle, looking in on each inhabitant.

Emily is too pathetic, Samantha is paralysed, Sarah looks at him heroically, and Max looks at him defiantly. This leaves Alex and Scott. Alex is sitting in a corner of his cubicle with his legs pulled up and his forearms draped across his knees nonchalantly as if he is taking all of this in his stride. Scott is just starting to wake up, stirring in his sleep. Richard did not realize how hard he hit him behind the head and now the kid probably has a concussion.

Richard stops in front of Scott. He yells loudly, his voice bounces off the concrete walls, "Wake up!"

Hurriedly Scott sits up and scoots himself across the floor to the corner of the room. He looks up in terror. "Let me go. You don't understand, my sister is all alone."

"Get up." Richard stares down at the boy.

Slowly, Scott lifts himself off the ground and then pushes his back further against the wall behind him. He

pulls his hand up protectively until it jerks back, and he notices his hand is cuffed to a chain, which is connected to a metal ring in the floor.

Warningly Richard says, “Stand still. I have a job for you.”

Scott stands still until Richard pulls the dog training choke chain over his head. Scott pulls away, but it is too late, the chain around his neck tightens quickly and cuts into his skin, choking his breath out of him.

Richard pulls Scott behind him, while Scott investigates each cubicle as he stumbles past them. He sees other kids look out at him with dirty faces and huge eyes.

Richard hands Scott a shovel and a bucket and then he leads him around to each cubicle to clean it. Scott gags every time he scoops the human excrement from the ground and drops it into the bucket.

When the foul mess has been shovelled up from the floor, he tells Scott to put the bucket by the foot of the steps. He hands Scott a bucket with soapy water and a mop.

Silently and slowly Richard follows Scott around the room as he mops up the remaining dirt and pee stains.

When Sarah or Max dare look him in the eye, he storms at them threateningly and afraid they avert their eyes quickly.

When the room is as close as it will ever again get to a fresh pine smell, he orders Scott to pick up the bucket and shovel as well. The unfortunate kid can hardly manage with two buckets, a shovel and a mop, but he stumbles up the stairs in front of Richard while the choke chain bites into the soft skin around his neck painfully.

Outside, Richard orders Scott to tip the soap-water into a ditch and then Richard takes the bucket from Scott. He twirls the bucket above his head and then when he lets go of the black plastic handle, the pink plastic bucket flies in a high, majestic curve across the soft pale blue of the early morning sky. It almost reaches above the trees, but then it brushes against the very top of a tree and it twirls and swirls in its plummet back to earth.

Richard pulls Scott to the back of the cabin. He says abruptly, "Take the shovel and dig a hole."

Obediently, Scott starts to scoop the soft, dark brown soil. He is not sure how deep or how long he has to make the hole and panicked he wonders if he is digging his own grave.

After twenty minutes, Richard laughs amused. He has been watching the nervous expression on the little boy's face and he could not help imagining all the frightening thoughts rushing through his head. "Bury the shit bucket."

Scott drops the bucket down the hole and when it hits the bottom with a sickening slopping noise, the smell wafts up.

Richard exclaims as he gasps for air, "Fuck." He lets go of the choke chain as he steps further away from the stinking hole. "Cover the hole," he bellows. "And don't get ideas and think you can run. There is nowhere to go."

After Scott has covered the hole, Richard drags him behind him toward a rainwater container on four wooden stilts to the side of the back garden. With clothes and all he pushes Scott into an outdoor shower cubicle and then he turns on the tap. The water rattles through the pipes directly from the rainwater drum, and then the ice-cold water gushes over Scott's head. He has an instant brain freeze, and his lungs battle to find a breath of air.

Richard lets him stand under the water for two full minutes, but to Scott it feels like two hours.

Laughing amused, Richard turns off the tap, and then

he yanks Scott out of the cubicle.

Rivulets of water run down Scott and puddle in every footprint he leaves in the soft soil.

They walk back to where Scott let the spade lean against the side of the cabin. For a moment, Scott considers grabbing onto the wooden handle of the shovel and hitting Richard over the head with it. Richard is as big as a bear though, and fearfully Scott considers he would have to hit him more than once.

Without making a grab for the shovel, he stumbles past it. They enter the cabin and then Richard lets Scott use the toilet. He keeps the door open and stands with his legs spread apart, his body braced should the kid decide to make a run for it.

When Scott is finished, he comes walking out of the little room meekly. Richard pulls him back to the stairs and down to the basement, where after he chains him to the floor again.

Richard takes each kid up individually. He lets them each have a two-minute freezing cold shower and then he leads them to the toilet to do their business.

Lastly, he takes Sarah. As Sarah is pulled roughly with

the choke chain pinching into her flesh, she looks around curiously. She looks for opportunities which might present themselves. She counts the stairs and her steps from the door to the shower. Her eyes fall on the shovel standing up straight against the outside wall of the cabin. Her eyes take in every detail of the cabin she can see as Richard leads her to the toilet.

Richard sighs when at last he finished his chores. He cleaned them, took them on a bathroom run, and filled their bowls with kibble and clean, fresh water from the tap.

He slumps down onto the couch in front of the TV exhausted.

EIGHT

Richard is half asleep, half awake. The whole exercise of this morning has him worn out. Also, during the last week he had not had a lot of sleep with watching and following their prey, studying and writing exams. It is now starting to take its toll and he is happy that by next week he will be able to just sit back and take a break before he must go home for Thanksgiving. He is not looking forward to it, his mother married his third stepfather four months ago, and judging by the last two, he can only imagine the fun and games awaiting him. He is no longer a sad, weak little boy who had just lost his dad in a horrific car accident, a boy who is an easy target for a man with

quick fists. No. That little boy is grown up now and will give back as good as he receives.

When Gareth arrives at the cabin, he pushes the hooter twice and Richard comes walking out of the front door, still a little dazed, between sleep and wakefulness.

Gareth laughs friendly when he sees him, "You having a good sleep in the middle of the day?"

"I just dozed off a little. It is about time you get here."

"The shops were busy, and I had to stand in an hour-long line to buy the supplies. Help me get the stuff inside."

They carry the shopping bags inside and leave them standing on the kitchen counter. They each pull a beer from the pack and then they sit down on the couch, next to each other.

"Give me a moment to catch my breath, and then we will start with the video."

Richard throws back his head as the golden liquid rushes down his throat. He swallows the cool, refreshing liquid. "Will it be uploaded by this afternoon?"

"Easy."

"Good. I cannot wait for the most important part to start."

Richard walks down the steps and when he gets down into the basement, he says with an excited voice, "Okay. So, who is first?"

The tension in the room is palpable.

He walks into the first cubicle randomly, and he starts to unlock Max from his handcuffs. He takes the chain in his hand, twirling it around his fist and then he orders Max to stand up while the kid looks up at him nervously.

He pushes Max in the back hard, and Max stumbles as he tries to regain his footing. Richard nudges Max up the stairs forcefully.

When they reach the upstairs lounge area, he shoves Max onto a chair in front of a white sheet strung across a line pulled taut across the length of the room.

Max sits down in the high back chair and moves his bottom backward so that his back sits up straight with the back of the chair.

Then only does he notice Gareth, sitting behind the large flat screen computer monitor.

Gareth angles the webcam while he keeps his eyes on the monitor in front of him until he finds the perfect perspective.

Max is centred in the screen; the lighting is perfect. His black hair is long and curls up above his ears and in his neck. There are light freckles speckled across his nose, and his big grey eyes are huge and framed darkly in long lashes. His eyes are dull and sad and tell a story of heart-breaking despair.

Gareth says in a soft, encouraging voice, "You are the only one here whose name we do not know."

Max says uncertainly, "Max."

"So Max, tell us your story. Why were you living on the streets?"

"It's personal."

"Let me explain why you are here." Gareth pauses and looks at Max thoughtful. Max feels reluctantly as if this young man cares about his well-being. "You have been carefully selected by us to participate in our online reality show. I predict this video I will be uploading later today will go viral and it will without a doubt be a worldwide internet sensation."

Max frowns as he looks back at Gareth uncertainly.

Gareth continues in a quiet voice, "You have to make me, and the world believe you should be the one who wins

at the end of the six-day run. You have to convince us why you are the perfect youngster and why you should be victorious, above the other five kids down in the basement."

Max interrupts him, "What do I win?"

Richard laughs boisterously from the kitchen area, where he is leaning against the kitchen counter, drinking another beer.

Gareth smiles enigmatically. "Well, Max, it is really up to you. How much is your life worth to you? Does it have the same worth as a million dollars, or maybe a recording contract, fame and fortune?"

Unsure Max asks softly, "My life depends on this?"

Gareth nods his head. "It sure does, so I suggest you make a compelling argument of why viewers should choose you." Gareth looks at the screen in front of him again and fiddles with the webcam facing Max a little bit more. When he looks up at Max again, he says, "So? Shall we start again? Why were you living on the streets, Max?"

Max moves himself back on the chair uncomfortably. "My name is Max and I am nine years old. My mom left me and my dad when I was four years old, so it used to be

just me and my dad. My dad has an evil temper and sometimes he will wake up in a foul mood. Usually I stay out of his way, but sometimes I can never tell what it would be that will trigger his mood swing from being happy and smiling to hitting me with the back of his hand across my face." Max stops nervously and looks down at his hands twined together tightly in his lap. Uneasily he fingers a long scar across the palm of his right hand. He wonders if he should say it, will it make people choose him. He continues with a stutter, "Before my gran died, she once told me I am too young to know for sure, but I like boys more than I like girls."

Gareth asks amused, "You mean you are gay?"

Ashamed Max lowers his head even further. It is as if he shrinks into himself, and he says, barely audible, "Yes."

Gareth chuckles. "So, speak up, Max. Be proud and announce it to the world."

Defiantly Max lifts his head and speaks directly into the webcam, his eyes do not waver from the conspicuous lens. "My dad kicked me out of the house just after I turned seven years old because I am gay. I decided then that living on the streets, scavenging for food and shelter is better

than living with him. I am not sure what constitutes a perfect young person, but I would hope choosing to live the way you want to live even though it might be difficult would be a good quality to have."

Gareth smiles as he hovers the mouse over the screen and clicks the pause button. "Perfect Max, you will get my vote."

Richard moves closer and pulls Max up by his arm roughly. He twists the chain hanging from Max's arm around his hand again until it pulls tight. Prodding Max every now and again in the small of his back, he pushes him to the bathroom.

Brusquely he instructs Max, "Use the loo and be quick about it."

The door to the little room remains a little ajar, and Max struggles to use the toilet, with his arm being pulled awkwardly away from his body.

When Max comes out of the room, Richard grabs him by the scruff of the neck and shoves him back to the door leading down into the basement.

After Richard shackles Max to the floor in his own private cubicle again, he moves to the cubicle next door

and he unlocks Alex.

He prods Alex in the back. Slowly they walk up the stairs. The muscles in Richard grow stiff as he prepares himself should Alex try to swing back at him or try to make a run for it. Alex is as meek as a lamb though and walks up the stairs in front of Richard obligingly.

Alex knows his dad is already out there looking for him, and he believes with all the money his dad has, it will only be moments before the entire police force breaks through the doors and windows to rescue him.

Upstairs Alex sits down onto the chair without Richard having to push him down into it.

Again, Gareth angles the webcam until he has Alex in the centre of the screen. The light shines perfectly on his flawless features. Blond hair - perfectly trimmed in the latest fashion. Green eyes with hazel flecks, and an easy smile which lights up his eyes. He has a faultless nose, above full rose-red lips, which rest upon a strong jaw.

"So, Alex, tell us what makes you the perfect teen."

"My dad will hunt you down and kill you. You made a big mistake making me drunk and then abducting me."

"Now, now, let's not get all worked up." Gareth smiles

sarcastically. "We are all here now, so let's make the best of it," Gareth repeats the story he told Max earlier of why they are here, and how Alex's life depends on him convincing the viewers to choose him above the other five.

Kindly Gareth says, "So, shall we start again? What makes you the perfect teen, Alex?"

Alex squares his shoulders and he boasts, "I am a football star at my school, with scouts phoning and trying to sign me daily. I have a bright future ahead of me and I am living the American dream. My life is like a high school musical and I am the star."

Gareth looks at him reproachfully across the monitor, and he recognizes most of the qualities and personality traits in Alex are the same as his own. He thinks he has everything, but in fact he has nothing.

Gareth asks amused, "Anything else to convince the viewers why they should choose you?"

"No. People aren't stupid, and they will choose me because I am the perfect teen."

"Okay then." Gareth nods his head at Richard, who is standing off to the side. "I am done with this one. Do not

bring any more, I think we should let them go up into the contest two at a time. We only have thirty seconds for each video, and I doubt I will be able to make an effective video if we try to put all six of them in all at once."

Alex asks, "Am I up against that gay-boy?"

Gareth frowns as he says, "Yes, you are."

Alex smiles, pleased. "Easy win."

Richard yanks him up out of the chair. He feels agitated with the boastfulness of Alex and deep down he wishes he gets voted off first, he will enjoy killing this one.

Richard pulls the chain around Alex's arm roughly and pulls him to the basement door.

Gareth laughs amused. "Richard, toilet first."

Richard considers this for a moment and then reluctantly he pulls Alex toward the bathroom roughly.

When Alex goes into the little room, he pushes the door closed, although it would not close properly because the metal chain is in the way.

Kicking the door open, Richard hisses, "Just do it. You have nothing I want."

Richard leans against the wall facing away from the open bathroom door. When Alex comes walking out of

the room, he pushes him ahead of him back to the basement. As they walk down the stairs, Richard suppresses the urge to kick Alex in the small of his back to send him sprawling down the stairs.

He locks the chain onto the metal ring in the floor with the industrial padlock again, and then methodically he fills the water and food bowls, ignoring the eyes looking up at him silently, pleadingly. When he walks into Emily's cubicle she scurries across the concrete floor and cringes in the corner.

As he switches off the light, after he is finished with his tasks, he smiles when Emily cries out in panic. When he was little, he had to learn quickly that there are no monsters in the pitch black of your bedroom, the monsters walk around all day long in broad daylight. Monsters do not hide away in dark corners. They prey on the lonely rich widowed women with young kids.

When he gets upstairs, Gareth is hunched in front of the computer screen, his eyes are focused on the images, and his finger clicks wildly on the mouse as he moves it across the mouse pad.

Richard sits down and clicks the remote control to

switch on the television. He settles down into the couch as he watches a horror movie about a normal alligator, which lived in a normal swamp, but then pollution leaked into his habitat and now the alligator has grown to monstrous proportions and has developed an unquenchable hunger for human flesh.

As the credits roll up onto the screen, Gareth gives a long-satisfied sigh. “Finished. Come look.”

Richard gets up off the couch and walks around to Gareth. He stands behind Gareth and wait for him to click the play icon.

Ominous piano music starts playing on a black screen, and then with an explosion of sound, a yellowish skull exPLODES out of the black background. The words: The Death Factor shimmer above and below the skull.

Richard recognizes the voice, but it is distorted and sounds like it is coming from the bottom of a deep pit. The voice announces excitedly, “Six days, six contestants and only one survivor. Which one of them will win the ultimate price, their life? Who will be your favourite? Is it the homeless nine-year-old boy with the freckles across his nose and the big, sad eyes?”

Ten seconds of the edited video show Max announcing he is gay and that his father kicked him out of the house because of this.

The voice continues, "Or will it be the handsome high school football hero?" Ten seconds play across the screen as Alex boasts he is the leading star in his own high school movie. The anonymous voice implores eagerly, "Remember, your vote is important, so vote now by entering your contestant's number in the comments hereunder." The video fades to black.

Excitement fills Richard. "That's perfect."

Gareth connects to the internet with the disposable cell phone he bought using Richard's dead father's name. He knows by doing this he has implicated Richard, because the police will quickly realize the connection to Richard, but he has already purchased a fake passport for himself, withdrawn most of his money from his trust fund, and packed it in the false bottoms of his three suitcases.

All of this is waiting for him in the trunk of his car at the airport. After he leaves the cabin at the end of this week, he is going to disappear forever. When the police apprehend Richard, Gareth will be long gone, living a new

life with a new identity.

He loads the video onto their fake video channel and then he moves away from the desk. As he stands up, he pushes his palms in the small of his back as he stretches the stiffness from being hunched forward for so long.

Richard says disappointed, “It is such a damn shame we will never get recognition for this.”

Gareth smiles. “A little lesson I learned from my father is things done in secret gives you the biggest satisfaction.”

The next morning, the first thing Richard does, is rush to the computer. He does not know the password, so he urges Gareth to, "Hurry up."

Gareth enters the long, encrypted password and then after he connects to the internet, he opens their video channel.

Disappointed Richard notices they have only had two thousand views, and most of the comments are insulting and derogatory. There are some votes with smiley faces after them.

Richard sulks, "Nobody is taking us seriously."

Gareth consoles him, "They will tonight after we add

the extra five seconds. I told you by the end of this week this video will be viral, and people are still sharing it. You cannot become an internet sensation overnight."

"Get a pen and paper," Gareth tells Richard.

When Richard comes back, Gareth reads the votes from the hundred or so people who jokingly voted for either Max or Alex. Richard writes the numbers in two columns.

After they reach the end of the comments, they lean their heads closely together and add the numbers.

Disappointed Richard leans back as Gareth says laughingly, "Well, well, who would have thought the boastful Alex will get more votes than the poor Max. I thought Max would get all the sympathy votes."

Richard says upset, "The kid did not have a fair chance."

"Yes, but we have a plan we must stick to, and unfortunately we cannot break our own rules. The one with the lowest number of votes are out of the competition."

Hopeful Richard asks, "Maybe we as producers can have a mercy vote."

Gareth laughs heartily. "No. We have to add the five seconds today, so people take us seriously."

Richard sighs. "You're right, but I really wanted that Alex out of the way."

Gareth considers that for two years he and Richard have been roommates, and in all that time they have been friends, never did he ever get the feeling Richard does not like him, yet here Richard is now loathing Alex, who has the same arrogant nature as Gareth. Gareth feels proud of himself for being able to hide his true character, to pretend to be charming and enigmatic, instead of being conceited.

Gareth asks, "So how are we going to do this. Who is going to tape the killing and who is going to do the deed?"

Unsure Richard hesitates. He does not mind being rough, to be violent and forceful, but he does not know if he will be able to actually kill someone.

Gareth says, "My hand is steadier than yours for the camera work."

With a sigh Richard says, "How are we going to do it? I suppose we are in it already; it is not as if we can let them go after the six days with a lollipop and a pat on the back."

They spend the next half an hour sitting across from

each other and discussing various methods of murder. Distractedly Gareth nibbles on a breakfast biscuit while Richard eats a bowl of cereal when they finally decide on the most gruesome method to boost their viewing numbers.

They dump the coffee mugs and dishes in the basin and then Richard starts the ritual of bringing each one of them upstairs to use the toilet.

Exhausted, he slumps down on the couch after he takes the last one back down to the basement. "You would think someone with as much money as your dad would have installed a toilet down there by now."

"He does not think about anything other than making money. If it does not inconvenience him, it is impossible it could ever be a problem for somebody else."

Richard gets up off the couch, and then in the kitchen, he gulps down two cans of beer in quick succession. He burps loudly. "Okay, let's do this. I'll fetch Max."

He pulls a protesting Max up the stairs. Richard yells loudly, "It is not my fault they did not vote for you. I had every faith in you to beat Alex, but you didn't, so shut the fuck up and move."

When they walk out into the quiet sunshine, Max gets a resolute look on his face and he pulls his shoulders square. He stops in the middle of a dusty clearing and bravely he keeps his head up. The metal chain is wrapped around his arms a few times. Even if he ran, he knew he would not get far.

Gareth opens the digital video camera and focuses on Max.

Richard moves to stand behind Max and then he swings the spade in a wide arc. The flat side of the spade hits the side of Max's head with a loud, dull noise.

Gareth zooms in to Max's face and videotapes his big, sad eyes go dull as all the life is sucked out of it.

Max slumps down to the ground in one fluid movement.

Richard steps over the lifeless body and bends down to take Max's feet. He takes a foot in each hand and then he drags the body across the light brown, dusty ground into the gathering of trees circling around the cabin.

When he walks back to Gareth he asks, "So who do you want to interview today?"

Gareth turns to him and they walk back to the cabin.

"Let's do Scott, the drug dealing kid and that disabled girl."

"They are both black though."

Richard laughs humorously. "That will keep it fair, won't it? We both know if a white kid had to go up against a black kid, the white kid will win hands down every time."

As soon as they walk back into the cabin, Gareth moves to the computer to upload the footage and to start editing the death of Max. Richard goes down the stairs to the basement.

He unlocks Scott and drags his skinny emaciated body up the stairs. He pushes him to the chair and then he bumps him so that Scott falls back onto the chair.

Gareth moves the webcam while keeping his eyes on the screen. When he has the perfect perspective of Scott, he looks pleased with himself. The lighting is perfect. Scott looks back at him on the screen. His big brown eyes look at him scared, and tears start to roll down his dirty cheeks, leaving glistening tracks on his brown skin.

Gareth explains to Scott why he is here and why it is important he states clearly why people should vote for him.

He looks across the room at Scott kindly and he smiles.

Scott looks back at Gareth and he smiles a nervous smile, his bottom lip quivers.

"So, Scott, why should people vote for you?"

His soft voice says quietly, "If I die my sister will be all alone. I do not sell drugs because I enjoy it. I do it because I have to, so I can feed my sister." The crumpled hundred-dollar bill in his pocket got him here in the first place, scratches against his thigh. "Please you have to let me go, my sister will be scared without me, my mom and dad is no good."

"Are your mom and dad your best customers, Scott?" Gareth asks with a smirk.

Scott lowers his eyes, embarrassed. "No, they can't afford what I sell. When I take the money I make, to my boss, he takes the drugs as well, so my parents can't steal it from me."

"Anything you want to add to plead for votes."

"My sister is still very young, and she has always only had me. Please. You must let me go."

Gareth smiles reassuringly. "You have my vote, Scott. Hopefully, the rest of the world will feel the same way."

Gareth nods his head to Richard, indicating he can take Scott back to the basement.

Richard feels sorry for the kid, so he walks him back to the basement after he takes him to the bathroom without pushing and prodding at him meanly.

He shackles Scott and then he walks across the narrow passage to Samantha's cubicle.

After he unlocks her, he throws her across his shoulder with a grunt. Uselessly, she hits her fists against his back while his arm wraps around her lifeless legs in front of his chest. He feels a shiver of disgust scamper down his spine at the thought of holding onto her dead legs.

Upstairs he puts her down on the chair, and he pulls her up so that she is sitting up straight on the chair.

Gareth is getting bored of telling the same story twice a day, but if he did not convince them of why they should give a compelling reason why they should be chosen as the perfect kid, everything he and Richard have done so far would be wasted and ineffectual.

He avoids looking directly at her accusing eyes as he tells her. While he speaks, he looks at the monitor, and he moves the webcam until he has the ideal image of her. Her

black dreadlocks frame her small, fragile face perfectly, and her full lips are naturally rose coloured.

He prefers to look at the virtual image of her, rather than the real image. It is more detached, and he does know this girl personally, have spoken to her many times. He knows she had a crush on him, like so many other girls.

After he explains the reason why she is here, he asks her image on the screen in front of him, "So why are you the perfect teen?"

She says nothing and her image stares back at him defiantly.

Exasperated, he sighs. "Sammy, come on. Don't you want to win this thing?"

She continues staring at him silently.

Ten minutes later, when Gareth cannot stand her accusing eyes boring into him any longer, he exclaims, "Fine! Richard, you can take this bitch downstairs again."

Richard hauls her over his shoulder roughly and then while she is hammering her fists against his back, he takes her back to her cubicle.

Like the afternoon before, he fills the water bowls and food bowls silently. He cannot suppress the urge when he

walks into Alex's cubicle and he kicks him hard against the shin.

Alex yells in pain and starts to rub his leg vigorously. "What the fuck you do that for?"

Richard kicks at him again, but Alex moves fast and out of the way of the large black combat boot.

Gareth calls his name and after a moment of hesitation while he considers going after Alex in the corner or not, he turns around and after he switches off the light, he walks up the creaking stairs.

He slams the basement door shut behind him, just as Gareth says, "Look, the views have gone up. It is nearly ten thousand already. I told you it takes time for people to catch on."

Richard rushes forward and peers down at the screen. He feels an immediate sense of accomplishment.

Gareth laughs, delighted. "Wait till we upload the piece with Max. It will sky-rocket."

Richard walks away to the kitchen to get a beer. "It is a pity we have to keep uploading a new video."

"I am going to add a link to the other video's page to the new video. So, as they finish watching the one, they

will click on the link and watch the new video." Delighted, he adds, "We might have more than one video go viral."

Richard slumps down in front of the TV and watches the screen without really watching anything. He is elated his wish is being fulfilled, but he is upset it must be anonymous. He needs the public acknowledgement that he has accomplished something everyone else with a video still wants to do.

Gareth edits the video and after half an hour he calls Richard to come and look.

"That was fast."

"I didn't have to do all the intro music and graphics again and I just added the two new edited videos onto the introduction I saved last night."

Richard watches the screen intently as the ominous piano music starts playing on a black screen, and then with an explosion of sound, a yellowish skull exPLODES out of the black background. The words: The Death Factor shimmer above and below the skull.

Again, the echoing voice announces excitedly, "Six days, six contestants and only one survivor. Who will win the ultimate price, their life? Who will be your favourite?

Is it the delinquent fourteen-year-old black kid who sells drugs on the street corner to feed him and his abused younger sister?"

Ten seconds of edited video show Scott, the tear tracks on his cheeks are clearly defined, as he begs for his life so he can take care of his sister.

The voice continues, "Or will it be the black disabled freshman college girl with a bright business career ahead of her?" Ten seconds play across the screen as Samantha stares defiantly back while the words—Please vote for me—scroll across the bottom of the screen.

The rasping voice says cheerfully, "Last night you saved Alex." A picture of Alex flashes across the screen. "But unfortunately, Max had to leave us and here is his swan song."

The camera follows the swoop of the spade in slow motion and then as it hits against Max's head and his head recoils slowly, the video cuts to Max's eyes as the light fades out of them.

The screen fills with red, blood-like graphics oozing from the top to the bottom and the words—Voted Out—flashes across the screen until the video fades to black. The

voice implores, “Your vote is important, so if you want your favourite to be the sole survivor you must vote.”

Richard smiles pleased. “It’s perfect.”

“I am going to upload it quickly and then add the hyperlinks to yesterday’s video.”

Gareth uploads the video and then he joins Richard in the kitchen.

Richard is frying a couple of eggs and bacon. They have been snacking on junk food all day and Gareth cannot wait to have a decent meal in his stomach for a change.

TEN

During the night, Sarah wonders, "What happened to Max? I have not heard his voice all day."

Samantha tells her what Gareth told her when she was upstairs, that they are part of an online reality show and whoever gets the lowest number of votes are then killed.

For the rest of the night, they do not speak. The consistent sound of Emily crying lulls them, and one by one they fall asleep reluctantly.

Richard and Gareth wake up long after lunch, after a night of heavy drinking.

The first thing they do is rush to the computer and

after Gareth enters the elaborate password, he links to the internet and then they open The Death Factor page.

Richard staggers as he notices the astonishing amount of two hundred and seventy-five thousand views.

Gareth exclaims excitedly, “I told you it is a brilliant idea.”

Viewers have started to take it seriously and after they sift through the nasty comments and the exclamations of outrage, they start counting the votes. The list feels endless, but two hours later the votes are in. Scott has been voted out.

Briefly Richard feels sorry for the kid, but he asks, “Do we do it the same way as yesterday?”

Gareth contemplates for a moment. “No, let’s lynch him instead. We have to keep it fresh.”

Richard goes down to the basement and then he drags a kicking and screaming Scott up the stairs behind him.

He says without any sympathy, “The viewers obviously do not approve of you selling drugs, even if you do it only to support your sister and because you were unlucky enough to have worthless parents.”

He drags Scott out the door into the open clearing and

then he forces the dog training choke chain around his neck. He adds a long rope to the end of the choke chain and then he flings it across a high branch. Scott starts to kick and scream loudly. Richard pulls the kid up by his neck while Gareth films his kicking legs. When Scott's legs start to spasm, he moves the camera up to his face. Soon dullness replaces the panic in his eyes.

Richard lets go of the rope and Scott drops down to the ground with a bone crushing sound. Richard drags the body into the dense undergrowth among the trees and leaves the body there—just far enough so it cannot be seen from the cabin and it is hidden among the lush foliage.

Richard and Gareth walk back to the cottage as if nothing untoward has happened, just part of a job, a means to fulfil a goal.

When they walk into the cabin, Gareth says, "Before we start today, let's eat something. I am starving this morning."

"I wish we could order a pizza."

"I brought some frozen pizza." Gareth walks to the freezer and then he pulls out two large boxes. He turns the

knob on the stove to the required heat setting and then he walks to the bathroom. He has a quick shower and then when he returns to the kitchen, the little pilot light has gone off indicating the oven has reached the correct temperature.

He takes the two pizzas from the boxes and then he slides them onto the rack. He calls down the short passage, "Hey, Richard. Where are you?"

"Here." The voice comes from the little room at the back. "Call me when you are ready. My head is killing me."

Gareth laughs as he walks to the computer to upload the video of Scott and to start editing it, while he waits for the pizza to cook.

Ten minutes later, he walks over to the stove and pulls open the door. The heat slams him in the face and as he pulls the pizza from the rack, his knuckle brushes against the rack. He pulls his finger back fast and then pops his finger in his mouth hurriedly. He grumbles in pain.

With his other hand, he pulls the pizza from the oven and puts them down onto the counter. He takes his finger from his mouth and examines his finger closely. A white crust has formed on the burn, and unhappily he breaks a

few slices from the pizza awkwardly with his one hand and only four fingers of his other injured hand.

He calls Richard loudly as he walks with the plate of pizza and a beer to the couch. After he sits down, he holds his burning finger against the cold beer can and he takes a bite of the pizza in his other hand.

Bleary eyed, Richard joins him on the couch with his own beer and plate of pizza.

They eat in silence until Richard asks, "What happened to your finger?"

"I burned the bloody thing pulling the pizza from the oven."

Richard shakes his head, amused. "You have always been a little clumsy."

Gareth mumbles displeased, "So my dad tells me every time I see him."

They finish eating and leave the empty cans and plates on the coffee table.

Richard says as he gets up from the couch, "I'll bring Emily up first."

In the meantime, Gareth walks to the computer. He sits down and puts his painful finger in his mouth again.

Emily screams at the top of her lungs as Richard carries her up the stairs. Her body is rigid as he holds her body horizontally in his arm.

He puts her down on the chair, but Emily jumps up immediately, trying to run away from Richard. Exasperated Richard lunges at her. He asks her in a booming voice, "Do you want to see your mother again?"

Immediately she stops screaming and she looks up at him hopefully.

He holds her up in front of him, so she is face to face with him. He looks at her and as he smiles kindly, he says, "If you help me and answer the questions, we are going to ask you, I promise you will see your mom again."

She looks across the room at Gareth, as she says accusingly, "You are Maria's friend and she really likes you."

Gareth ignores her as he edits the video, trying to get the images of Scott just right.

Richard asks her, "So are you going to be good or must I tie you to the chair?"

She nods her head. "I'll sit still."

He puts her down on the chair, but he stays close by,

just out of camera range.

Gareth focuses the webcam on her. She looks heartbreakingly sad with her big scared eyes. Her blonde pigtails hang on the sides of her cheeks.

He asks her kindly, "So Emily, tell us what your biggest wish is."

Emily wails, "I want my Mommy and I am scared of the dark." She looks pleadingly at Gareth across the room. "Please tell this man to leave the lights on."

Gareth smiles as he looks up at Richard standing next to Emily. "Leave the lights on from now on. I think that is all we will need from Emily. You can bring Sarah up now."

"So, will you take me to see my Mommy now?"

Garth smiles sweetly at her. "Tomorrow. I promise."

She walks obediently next to Richard to the basement door. When they reach the door, she says innocently, "You know I am okay now and if you are taking me home tomorrow, you don't have to lock me up anymore. I'll be really, really good."

Gareth says from where he is still sitting in front of his computer, "Just for tonight, otherwise the other kids will

be jealous."

She nods her head in understanding and walks down the stairs in front of Richard.

After Richard secures Emily to the metal ring, she reminds him, "Remember, you have to leave the lights on."

Richard ignores her as he walks to Sarah's cubicle. He grimaces when he touches her wrist by accident. The dried blood, where she has tried to pull her hand through the handcuff turns into a rust coloured powder and clings to his sweaty hands.

He unlocks the other end of the handcuffs which are attached to the metal chain, which is connected to the metal ring in the floor. He pushes her roughly onto her stomach and then he cuffs her hands behind her back. He is tired, he has a headache, and he is not in the mood to fight her. The day he took them outside to clean them from their own filth, she tried to make a run for it, and he had to dive at her legs. His elbow is still a little tender to the touch.

He pushes her up the stairs ahead of him and she resists him with every step. Frustrated, he slaps her against

the back of her head. "Walk, before I beat you to a pulp."

Every time he shoves her in the back, she pushes back. He grabs onto the handcuffs and he yanks down hard.

Sarah gives a long scream of pain as the metal digs through the thick scab which has formed around her raw wrist.

Eventually, Richard gets her upstairs and onto the chair. He remains standing close to her with a baseball bat in his hand. He stands in the correct stance and he says warningly, "I swear if you get off that chair, I will hit your head clean off your shoulders and hit a home-run with your ugly face."

Sarah looks up at him mockingly.

Gareth has regretted the impulsive moment when he decided to grab Sarah from the street rather than to go with the girl who was initially their choice.

He focuses the webcam on her. To Richard, he says, "Turn her sideways, so the bruise on her eye is hidden from the camera."

Richard uses one hand to turn her with the chair. The other arm holds the bat up menacingly.

"I only need a photo from you, feisty Sarah. We already

have your interview on tape." He laughs cruelly. "You know, of course, you are going up against sweet little Emily, and with those huge sad eyes, I doubt you will get any votes. Hope you enjoy your last hours—any requests?"

Sarah stares at him with a murderous glare in her eyes. Her mind starts to work faster. She remembers every detail of the area outside the cabin. If they are going to kill her, surely, they will do it outside. She scans the room quickly and she cannot see any evidence of a struggle, so they did not kill Max or Scott in here. She has thought through every detail of an escape plan during their next bathroom visit, but every idea had too many pitfalls.

Richard takes her down and he pushes her down the last two steps. Sarah stumbles and with both her arms tied behind her back, she cannot manage to get her balance. She twists her body and slams with her shoulder onto the floor. She closes her eyes tightly and she groans loudly, as the pain shoots through her.

Richard picks her one leg up from the floor and then he drags her across the concrete to her cubicle. While he locks her securely to the metal ring again, he mumbles

close to her ear. "I hate girls like you. You toy with boys until they fall in love with you and then you move on to your next victim."

Sarah lifts her free hand to slap him, but he grabs her wrist and squeezes until he feels the bones move slightly in his grip. He lets go and she starts to rub her wrist while she looks up at him hatefully.

He walks away laughing wildly and then he switches off the light.

Emily screams in alarm. "You promised."

"I lied," he replies mockingly.

When he gets back upstairs, Gareth looks at him surprised. "That was quick. Did you feed them?"

"I am not in the mood tonight. I am going to lie down again, call me when you are done with the video."

Gareth calls after him, "Have another beer, it will take your headache away."

"Maybe later."

Gareth works on the video and he takes his time, because Richard is not in the room, glancing at him anxiously every five minutes.

After midnight, it is perfect, and he gets up from the

chair to stretch his back. He walks down the short passage to call Richard.

Richard is fast asleep; his mouth is hanging open slightly and a rhythmic soft gurgling snore escapes his mouth.

He nudges Richard against the shoulder, and he jerks upright. His arms shoot up in a defensive action.

Gareth laughs hysterically. "That's funny. Is the dead chasing you in your sleep?"

Bewildered Richard realizes where he is and he asks sleepily, "I suppose you finished the video."

"I have, come and look at it before I upload it."

Richard watches as the same ominous piano music starts playing on a black screen, and then with an explosion of sound, a yellowish skull exPLODES out of the black background. The words: The Death Factor shimmer above and below the skull.

The hollow voice announces excitedly, "Six days, six contestants and only one survivor. Who will win the ultimate price, their life? Who will be your favourite? Is it the heartbreakingly sad eight-year-old girl with the blonde pigtails?"

Ten seconds of the edited video show Emily asking repeatedly in her soft, lilting voice for her Mommy, and if she could please go home.

The voice continues, "Or will it be the pretty brown-haired teen homecoming queen?" Ten seconds play across the screen as Sarah smiles at the camera shyly where she stands on a suburban sidewalk and she tells the camera excitedly how she wouldn't say she is the perfect teen, but she likes to think she is close to being perfect. The video fades to the photo Gareth took of her earlier today. Her solemn face looks sad, as her dark eyes glare at the lens defiantly. The bruise on the side of her face looks like a shadow. The grating voice continues cheerfully, "Your votes saved Samantha last night." A picture of Samantha flashes across the screen. "Sadly, Scott was voted out and he paid dearly with his life." The camera is focused on two feet in dirty worn trainers. As the legs start to spasm violently, the camera pans up to the boy's face and focus on his eyes as the life is drained from them. The screen again fills with red, blood-like graphics oozing from the top to the bottom and the words—Voted Out—flashes across the screen until the video fades to black. The voice

implores, "Your vote is important, so if you want your favourite to be the sole survivor you must vote."

Curiously Richard remains standing behind Gareth as he connects to the internet. When he opens The Death Factor page, they both catch their breath simultaneously. The view count is one million four hundred and fifty-four thousand.

Richard exclaims, "Yes!" Never in his wildest imagination could he ever have imagined it would reach above one million views.

ELEVEN

They stay up all night, checking the view numbers every now and again.

When the night turns to day outside the cabin, Richard and Gareth are still staring at the screen in front of them incredulous. During the night, the views on their video channel grew to three million, seven hundred and eighty-six thousand.

Gareth whispers in awe. "It will take too long to count all these votes."

Richard cannot move his eyes away from the numbers. Every time the page refreshes the number increases by a thousand.

Gareth nudges him roughly. "I said we cannot count all these votes. Who do you want to kill today? You have the final vote."

Richard doubts he will be able to kill Emily if he is sober, and he still has a nauseated feeling from the night before last, when they stayed up until the early morning hours bulldozing through the supply of beers. He says without hesitation, "Sarah is my choice. I cannot stand her anyway. She and that Alex should have been voted off first."

Gareth agrees, "So Sarah it is. Are we going to do it now? I do not want to leave everything as late as yesterday and I want to go and sleep for a few hours."

"The quicker we do it, the faster we can move on to the semi-final round."

"How are you going to do it today?"

"I think I should follow through on my threat of yesterday. See if I can knock her head clean off her shoulders with the baseball bat."

Gareth laughs cruelly and then when he manages to take a breath of air, he asks, "Who shall we interview this afternoon?"

Richard thinks about it for a moment, and then he says, "Well, we have to put Alex up, it is his turn and he will have to go up against Samantha or Emily. Both the girls have the sympathy votes, so I feel sorry for the self-appointed star of his very own melodrama."

Grinning widely, Richard leaves a laughing Gareth in the lounge as he walks down the stairs into the dark, dank basement.

After he switches on the dim light, he walks over to her cubicle. "Told you your end will come today. Hope you had enough time to make peace with your maker." He laughs loudly at his own wittiness.

He pulls her up off the floor cruelly and then he takes the empty handcuff, which he unlocked from the chain and he cuffs her hands together in front of her. She will be dead soon, and he does not feel like going through the extra trouble of man-handling her onto the ground so he can cuff her hands together behind her back.

She walks in front of him and he shoves her toward the door, and then out of the door until she is standing in the middle of the clearing.

Gareth leans against the Jeep and he focuses the

camera on her head.

Richard stands behind Sarah. He bends his knees slightly and lifts the bat over his head. He steps back and makes a few practice hits before he steps closer to her again.

"Fuck," Gareth exclaims exasperated.

Richard lets the bat rest on his shoulder as he looks across the clearing toward Gareth. "What?"

"I forgot to charge the battery last night. Wait here while I quickly go inside to fetch the spare." He runs across the dry, dusty clearing.

Sarah realizes this will be her one and only opportunity to escape. As she bunches her hands together tightly, she looks back across her shoulder until she can see Richard from the corner of her eye. He is staring intently at the door into which Gareth has disappeared. She notices he is standing close enough behind her. With lightning speed, she twirls around, and her hands connect loudly with his temple. The metal cuffs cut a gash across his cheek. She hit him in the precise soft spot on the side of his eye, and he falls onto his knees. For a moment, she panics when it looks as if he is struggling to get up again. She urges her

legs to run.

Richard is standing on his hands and knees. The world is swirling in front of him in black and white concentric circles. He tries to get up, but his legs buckle under him. He takes a deep breath and shakes his head from side to side to try and clear the dizziness. He feels nauseous.

Sarah turns and runs into the trees surrounding the clearing. Bushes slap against her arms and face painfully. She stumbles over the foliage growing wild on the ground under her feet, but she continues to run as fast as she can.

When Gareth walks out of the cabin, he squints against the glaring bright sunlight. With shock, he sees Richard kneeling on his hands and knees, his head hanging between his arms.

He yells, "Which way did she go?"

Richard vomits loudly and spews bile onto the ground in front of him.

Panicked Gareth realizes Richard probably did not see in which direction she went. She could have run into the forest at a wide variety of angles and he would not know which way to go to follow her. The main road is five miles away and circles around, so it does not matter which

direction she chose, she will eventually get to the main road and depending how fast she is running and how fit she is, she could reach the road in as little as five hours—barely enough time for him to drive to the airport, to get his bags from the trunk of his car and to be on an airplane.

He runs back into the cabin hurriedly. He grabs the car keys hastily from the small table next to the door and then he dashes across the clearing to the Jeep. He gets in quickly and starts the engine. The car leaps and bounds under him as he drives around, across the rough patches of grass at the edge of the trees. He drives away from the cabin as fast as he can, the dust billowing up behind him.

From a distance, Sarah hears the engine of a car and scared she runs even faster. She continues running until her every breath rip from her lungs. She slows down and once her breath becomes more even and she does not have to wheeze for every mouthful of air, she hears the welcome music of car tires on tarmac. Not just one car, but many cars. She stumbles tired across fallen tree trunks, following the sound and then without warning, she stumbles out of the forest and onto the road. A car swerves wildly to avoid her and she lifts her shackled

hands up in the air, waving down the next car.

The man in the next car looks at her shocked and Sarah turns to watch him as he drives past her, but then he swerves his car onto the side of the road as he slows down to a stop.

She stumbles to the stationary car, and when the strange man gets out of his car, she cries croaky, "Please help us."

The man rushes to her and then he helps her to sit down on the side of the road. He pulls his cell phone from his pocket and then she hears the familiar sound of his fingers pressing the numbers 9-9-9.

TWELVE

Two days later, in an obscure corner of the world, Gareth pulls his laptop closer to him where he is sitting in a luxurious coffee shop. He switches it on and then he opens The Death Factor video page. With a self-satisfied smile he notices the views of the channel have reached a staggering fourteen million views. It will be difficult for any newcomer to beat that number. The page refreshes and then the message—Error 404 The page you requested does not exist—appears on the screen. Disappointed Gareth realizes the owners of the website removed the page, just as he opened it and frustrated, he considers if he should have taken a screenshot while he still had the

chance.

Gareth watches the news religiously whenever he gets the chance during the next two days and he knows Richard is in jail, and he will remain there for the rest of his mortal life. There is a massive manhunt under way for Gareth, but he knows they will never find him, not with his new identity.

He wonders amused if Richard knows he has accomplished his goal and he will be remembered forever as the most infamous internet sensation ever in the history of the internet.

Richard has attained life-long notorious status.

He did say he would even sell his soul.

Thank you for reading this story.
For more stories written by Stephen, please visit
www.stephensimpsonbooks.com

Printed in Great Britain
by Amazon